Baby Tamer

EGGMONT
family
CIRCUS
COMING SOON!

THRILLS!

SPILLS!

Mark Teague

SCHOLASTIC INC.
New York Toronto London Auckland Sydney

To Joseph

ISBN 0-590-95883-6

12 11 10 9 8 7 6 5 4 3 2 1   8 9/9 0 1 2 3/0

Printed in the U.S.A.   24

First Scholastic paperback printing, April 1998

The display type was set in Improv.
The text type was set in Sixpack.
The illustrations in this book were painted in acrylics.
Design by Marijka Kostiw

The baby-sitter, Amanda Smeedy,

showed up at six-fifteen.

She'd come to watch the Eggmont kids,

Clarabelle, Zeke, and Baby Lurleen.

Their parents met her at the door.
"Good luck, good luck!" they cried.
Then they turned and raced away
and were gone in the blink of an eye.

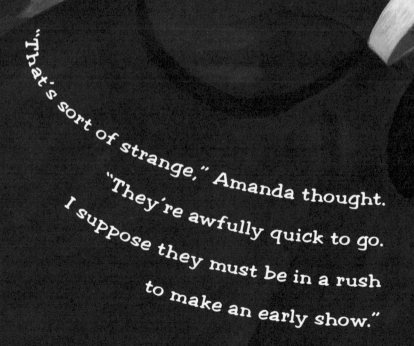

"That's sort of strange," Amanda thought.
"They're awfully quick to go.
I suppose they must be in a rush
to make an early show."

But once inside, Amanda gasped.
It was as wild as a circus in there.
The noise was enough to curl her toes
and send shock waves through her hair.

From bongo drums and fleegle horns

to piano and tambourine,

there was no louder three-piece band

than Clarabelle, Zeke, and Baby Lurleen.

Then Clarabelle did cartwheels,
while Zekey chased the cat.
And Baby Lurleen rode her choo-choo train
across the front door mat.

Amanda rubbed her chin and thought,
"They're merely trying to test me."
So she yawned and said, "Your little pranks
really don't distress me."

The Eggmont children sputtered and groaned.

This outcome wouldn't do!

If the baby-sitter yawned at Plan Number One,

it was time for Plan Number Two.

This plan called for greater mischief

on an even grander scale.

The Eggmonts cackled and clasped their hands.

This time they wouldn't fail!

Clarabelle quickly showed her skill
as a prankster and a teaser.
She dumped an octopus in the bath
and shoved penguins in the freezer.

Now came brother Zekey's turn,

and not to be outdone,

he jumped five chairs on his tricycle,

but crash-landed on the sixth one.

Then he performed his magic act.

He placed his top hat on a trunk

and mumbled secret magic words,

waved his wand – ta da! – a skunk.

Last of all came little Lurleen,
who walked a wire between two chairs,

then used the couch as a trampoline and disappeared up the stairs.

Amanda simply shrugged and said,

"I really must confess,

I've seen a lot of pranks before

and these just don't impress."

The Eggmonts howled and stamped their feet.

It was quite a sight to see.

But they still had one more plan to try:

The Big One, Number Three.

First Zekey set off fireworks.

They exploded rat-a-tat-tat!

And Lurleen charged through on a small white horse,

balancing like an acrobat.

Next came dancing elephants,

camels, monkeys, bears,

and Clarabelle the lion tamer,

with her flashing whips and chairs.

After all the uproar ended,

Amanda asked, "Isn't there more?"

But the Eggmont kids were too tired to move,

and they collapsed across the floor.

So she gathered the children one by one
and put them all to bed.

"You know, those pranks were pretty good,"
Amanda Smeedy said.

She ushered out the animals,

tidied up till the house was clean.

Then she kissed her sleeping friends good night,

Clarabelle, Zeke, and Baby Lurleen.

As she sat there eating ice cream,

she smiled, and who could blame her?

"I'm one cool cucumber," she told herself,

"AMANDA SMEEDY, BABY TAMER."